A Note to Parents

For many children, learning math is _____ ' is their first response — to which many parents silently add "Me, too!" Children often see adults comfortably reading and writing, but they rarely have such models for mathematics. And math fear can be catching!

The easy-to-read stories in this **Hello Reader! Math** series were written to give children a positive introduction to mathematics, and parents a pleasurable re-acquaintance with a subject that is important to everyone's life. **Hello Reader! Math** stories make mathematical ideas accessible, interesting, and fun for children. The activities and suggestions at the end of each book provide parents with a hands-on approach to help children develop mathematical interest and confidence.

Enjoy the mathematics!
• Give your child a chance to retell the story. The more familiar children are with the story, the more they will understand its mathematical concepts.
• Use the colorful illustrations to help children "hear and see" the math at work in the story.
• Treat the math activities as games to be played for fun. Follow your child's lead. Spend time on those activities that engage your child's interest and curiosity.
• Activities, especially ones using physical materials, help make abstract mathematical ideas concrete.

Learning is a messy process. Learning about math calls for children to become immersed in lively experiences that help them make sense of mathematical concepts and symbols.

Although learning about numbers is basic to math, other ideas, such as identifying shapes and patterns, measuring, collecting and interpreting data, reasoning logically, and thinking about chance, are also important. By reading these stories and having fun with the activities, you will help your child enthusiastically say "**Hello, math**," instead of "I hate math."

—Marilyn Burns
National Mathematics Educator
Author of *The I Hate Mathematics! Book*

For Kate and Dave,
who always kept our
cups full
— S.K.

For Kelly Welly,
Lindsay Bindsay,
and Ryan Fyan
— J.S.

Copyright © 2000 by Scholastic Inc.
The activities on pages 27-32 copyright © 2000 Marilyn Burns.
All rights reserved. Published by Scholastic Inc.
SCHOLASTIC, HELLO READER, CARTWHEEL BOOKS and associated logos are trademarks and/or registered trademarks of Scholastic Inc.

Library of Congress Cataloging-in-Publication Data

Keenan, Sheila.
    What's up with that cup?/ by Sheila Keenan; illustrated by Jackie Snider.
    p.   cm. — (Hello reader! Math. Level 2)
    Summary: While trying to make a piggy bank, a young girl learns the importance of using standard measurements. Includes related activities.
    ISBN 0-439-09954-4
    [1. Measurement—Fiction.   2. Stories in rhyme.]
    I. Snider, Jackie, ill.   II. Title.   III. Series.
    PZ8.3.K265Wj   2000
    [E]—dc21   99-20212
                                                           CIP

12 11 10 9 8 7 6 5 4 3 2 1   00 01 02 03 04

Printed in the U.S.A.   24
First Scholastic printing, February 2000

What's Up With That Cup?

by Sheila Keenan • Illustrated by Jackie Snider
Math Activities by Marilyn Burns

The Lum Collection

Hello Reader! Math — Level 2

Cartwheel
·B·O·O·K·S·®

SCHOLASTIC INC.
New York Toronto London Auckland Sydney
Mexico City New Delhi Hong Kong

Sally had a quarter.
Sally had a dime.
Sally lost her money
in almost no time.

It flew out of her pocket.
It disappeared with a splash.
Sally said, "I need a piggy bank
to hold my cash."

Sally couldn't buy a bank
without any dough.
She did have a book
that might help her, though.

Piggy Bank

1 balloon
newspapers
2 cups of warm water
1 cup of flour
paint

- Mix the flour and water to make a thick, creamy soup.
- Blow up the balloon.
- Tear the newspapers into strips.
- Dip the strips into the mixture.
- Wrap the strips around the balloon.
- Shape the pig's snout, ears, tail, and feet.
- Make a slit in the top and a hole in the bottom.
- Let dry, pop the balloon, and paint the pig.

21

Sure enough she found it,

"Piggy Bank," page 21.

She read the instructions and said,

"This will be fun!"

Sally found a spoon
and a big mixing bowl.
"I just need cups," she said,
"then I'm ready to roll."

She rummaged through every cupboard.

She rooted through every drawer.

She found plenty of cups,

but didn't know which to pour.

Since she needed more water than flour,
Sally took the biggest cup.
She held it under the faucet,
till it was all filled up.

Then Sally chose another cup,
the recipe did say two.
She thought, *This one is second biggest,
so it should do.*

Now Sally needed something else
to put the flour in.
She spotted a pretty teacup.
And brought it to the bin.

Sally started pouring
and mixing like mad.
This was the most
fun that she'd ever had!

After a few minutes,
Sally put down the spoon.
She took a deep breath
and blew up the balloon.

She shredded the newspaper
and picked up a strip.
"Here I go!" Sally said.
She started to dip.

Sally dipped the paper
into the bowl of goop
(which really didn't look
like a thick, creamy soup!)

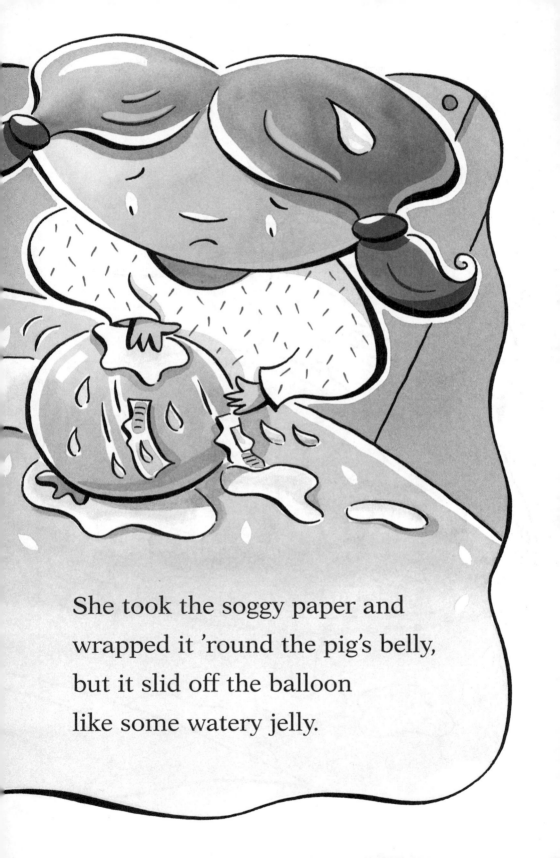

She took the soggy paper and
wrapped it 'round the pig's belly,
but it slid off the balloon
like some watery jelly.

Sally looked in the bowl and said,
"I really messed this up.
I'll start all over
with another cup."

Sally scooped the flour
into a big coffee cup.
She took toy cups to the sink
and filled them up.

Sally started mixing.
This was harder to stir.
Poof! Lots of flour
spilled all over her.

Sally said, "This is lumpy!
My spoon is stuck!"
She tried to dip the paper
without much luck.

She rinsed out the bowl
to give it another try.
But when she looked around,
she wanted to cry!

THERE WAS ONLY ONE CUP LEFT!

Sally just stood there with
flour on her nose.
She picked up the last cup —
and then she froze.

This cup was different.

It had writing on its side.

"One cup...," Sally read.

"I get it!" she cried.

"This is just what I need,
a measuring cup.
It will hold the same amount
each time I fill it up."

Sally used the same cup
three times over:
once for the flour
and twice for the water.

Sally stirred the goop and said,
"This time I won't fail."
She dipped the strips and
molded a pig from snout to tail.

"Look at this great bank!"
Sally said with pleasure.
"That sure was easy…

once I learned how to measure!"

• ABOUT THE ACTIVITIES •

Measurement is an important and practical part of mathematics. We measure the length of a hallway to see if a rug will fit, a cup of flour for a recipe, or children's heights to see how they've grown. We use a variety of tools to determine the size of things. Our purpose for measuring determines how accurate we need to be.

Young children are naturally interested in the sizes of things. For their first measuring experiences, they compare objects directly and identify them as bigger or smaller, longer or shorter, heavier or lighter, thicker or thinner. When children can't compare two objects directly, they typically find something to help them measure — sticks, containers, blocks, paper clips, or whatever else they have on hand. These tools give measurements that are non-standard and imprecise, but lay the foundation for children to learn about using standard measures and being more accurate.

Children learn about standard measures — cups, teaspoons, feet, pounds, and so on — by seeing that they serve an important purpose. *What's Up With That Cup?* focuses on a common standard unit of measure — one cup — and provides a familiar household context for using it. The story shows children how a standard measure can be important and useful.

The activities in this section give children experience with standard measures. Follow your child's interests and enjoy measuring together!

— Marilyn Burns

You'll find tips and suggestions
for guiding the activities whenever
you see a box like this!

Retelling the Story

When Sally was swinging, her money flew out of her pocket. She lost a quarter and a dime. How much money did Sally lose?

If your child hasn't yet learned the values of coins or how to count up money, you might be interested in *Monster Money* and *A Quarter from the Tooth Fairy*, Hello Reader! Math books that help with these skills.

Why did Sally think she needed a piggy bank?

To make the piggy bank, Sally needed to mix 2 cups of water and 1 cup of flour. She found a spoon and a big mixing bowl, but she didn't know which cups to use. What did Sally do then?

When Sally started putting the newspaper strips on the balloon, they slid off! What was the problem? Sally mixed another batch of flour and water, but it still didn't work. What happened this time?

What did Sally finally do to make the flour and water work right?

How Big Is a Cup?

Cups come in all sizes and shapes. Look in your kitchen cupboards and see what different cups you can find.

When you cook, a cup means one special kind of cup — a measuring cup. Find a measuring cup in your kitchen.

Which of the cups in your kitchen holds the same as a measuring cup? Which holds more? Less? Use a measuring cup and water to find out.

All About Spoons

Spoons come in all sizes and shapes, too. There are soup spoons, teaspoons, mixing spoons, and others. How many different size spoons do you think there are in your kitchen? See how many you can find.

When we cook, we use "measuring spoons," special spoons that measure specific amounts. Find a set of measuring spoons in the kitchen. The large one is called "one tablespoon." Then, in size order, there is "one teaspoon," "one-half teaspoon," and "one-quarter teaspoon."

How many of the largest measuring spoon (one tablespoon) do you think will fill one measuring cup with water? Try it and see.

Math Snack

Here's a recipe for making about 24 peanut butter balls. Put everything into a bowl and mix. Measure carefully! Then roll the balls using one teaspoon of the mixture for each.

Mix:

1 cup of peanut butter

1/2 cup of rolled oats

1/2 cup of powdered milk

1/2 cup of raisins

2 tablespoons of honey

The best way for a child to learn about standard measures is to have experiences using them. This recipe gives them experience both with a measuring cup and with measuring spoons.

Feet Count!

Try measuring across the kitchen floor with your feet. Count how many baby steps it takes you. Ask someone in your family to do the same.

People get different counts, because feet are different sizes. That's why we use a special "foot" when we need to measure. Find a ruler in the house that measures "one foot." (It will look like the one below, but straighter and bigger.) Use it to measure across the room. Now how many feet do you get?

Try some more measuring with your ruler.

How many feet across is the refrigerator? The kitchen table? The kitchen door or entrance?

Now try measuring yourself. How many feet tall are you?

Introducing a standard foot-long ruler helps give your child experience with an important standard measure of length.